NICK JR GO DIEGO GO!

LOOK AND FIND®

Animal Rescue Adventure

Illustrated by A&J Studios
Written by Caleb Burroughs

Published by Louis Weber, C.E.O., Publications International, Ltd.
7373 North Cicero Avenue, Lincolnwood, Illinois 60712

Ground Floor, 59 Gloucester Place, London W1U 8JJ

Customer Service: 1-800-595-8484 or customer_service@pilbooks.com

www.pilbooks.com

8 7 6 5 4 3 2 1

ISBN-13: 978-1-4127-6758-3
ISBN-10: 1-4127-6758-X

pi kids® **publications international, ltd.**

¡Hola! I'm Diego, and this is my sister, Alicia! We're Animal Rescuers. We rescue animals and take care of them here at the Animal Rescue Center. Do you see the gear we use on our rescue missions?

Rescue Pack

Video Watch

Field Journal

Sticky Gloves

Click

Spotting Scope

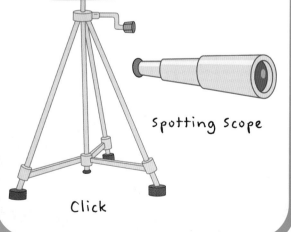

My whole family works at the Animal Rescue Center. We rescue lots of animals in the rainforest. See if you can find my family and my rainforest animal friends.

Papi

Baby Jaguar

Spectacled Bear

Mami

Alicia

Bobo Brothers

Sammy the Sloth

Animal Rescuers like me don't just rescue rainforest animals. I travel to many locations to help animals. I've helped lots of animals here at the beach. Will you find the animal friends I've helped that live on the sand or in the ocean?

Blue Shark

Harbor Seal

Leatherback Sea Turtle

Jellyfish

Seagull

Humpback Whale

Now let's go back to the rainforest, where lots of different animals live. Look for these baby rainforest animals and their mommies.

Howler Monkeys

Pygmy Marmosets

Jaguars

Spider Monkeys

Sloths

Maned Wolves

We also help animals who live high in the mountains. The air is thin and cold up here, but there are still lots of animals. Will you find these mountain animals?

Mami Jaguar

Linda the Llama

Chinchilla

Condor

Mountain Tapir

Puma

We also help animals all the way down in Antarctica, at the very bottom of the world! Brrr! It's really, really cold, but there are still lots of animals that live here. Try to find these Antarctic animals ... and those silly Bobo Brothers!

Bobo Brothers

Adelie Penguin

Chinstrap Penguin

Orca

Emperor Penguin

Sperm Whale

This is the desert. There's sand everywhere and it can get really, really hot during the day. But even though this is a hot and sandy place, many animals call the desert their home.

Prairie Dog

Roadrunner

Coyote

Tarantula

Bat

Rattlesnake

We made it back to the Animal Rescue Center. Click the Camera took a lot of pictures of the great places we went and all of the animals we saw — including a whole lot of baby animals! Will you look in the pictures here to spot these different baby animals?

Baby Spectacled Bear

Baby Puma

Baby Coyote

Baby Orca

Baby Caiman

Baby Leatherback Sea Turtle

Our adventures aren't over yet! Return to each scene and find these hidden things.

Animal Rescue Center

Look in the Animal Rescue Center to find some things that help us get around on our animal rescue missions.

Snowboard

Rubber Raft

Hang Glider

Zipcord

Hot Air Balloon

Kayak

The Rainforest

We take care of animals at the Animal Rescue Center and make sure they get everything they need to be happy and healthy. Swing back to the first rainforest page and find these things that both humans and animals need.

Food

Sleep

Water

Exercise

Shelter

The Beach

Let's think like Animal Scientists! We can find animals by spotting the different tracks they leave. Try to spot these different footprints and tracks at the beach.

The Bobo Brothers' Footprints

Diego's Footprints

Baby Jaguar's Footprints

A Sea Turtle's Tracks

A Seagull's Footprints

A Harbor Seal's Tracks

Back to the Rainforest

Go, Animal Scientists, go! Head back to the second rainforest page. Look closely and you'll see lots of animal homes, where they lay their eggs and raise their young. Try to spot these different kinds of eggs.

Blue Morpho Butterfly Eggs

Scarlet Macaw Egg

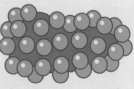

Caiman Eggs

Red-Eyed Tree Frog Eggs

The Mountains

It can be tough moving around in places that are rocky and cold. Climb back to the rocky, chilly mountains and look for these things that mountain animals and Diego use to get around and stay warm.

Climbing Boots

Parka

Climbing Rope

Eagle's Wings

Andean Mountain Cat's Thick Fur

Antarctica

Antarctica is a huge place. It's actually its own continent. Cruise back there to find these different ways to get around this giant land of ice and snow.

Dog Sled

Snowmobile

Snowshoes

Skis

Submarine

The Desert

Let's look closely, Animal Scientists! See if you can spot these other desert animals.

Jackrabbit

Scorpion

Desert Tortoise

Mexican Grey Wolf

Pocket Mouse

Tiger Salamander

Back to the Animal Rescue Center

Great! We've seen all kinds of different animals on our Animal Rescue missions. Will you count how many of each type of animal we have pictures of?

Reptiles (5)
Mammals (12)
Birds (6)
Swimming Animals (5)

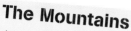